Rolling Along with Goldilocks and the Three Bears

Written by Cindy Meyers
Illustrations by Carol Morgan

Woodbine House   1999

Dedication

To Ken and our Goldilocks (Brittany) and
the three bears (Dustin, Keith, and Alec).
—Cindy Meyers

To Jim and Laura, for your love and
encouragement. Your Mom loves you.
—Carol Morgan

Once upon a time, there were three bears: a great big Papa Bear, a middle-sized Mama Bear, and a spunky little Baby Bear who used a wheelchair to get around. They lived in the forest in a house that had ramps instead of steps for Baby Bear.

There were three chairs in their home. There was a great big chair for Papa Bear, a middle-sized chair for Mama Bear, and a wee little chair for Baby Bear. Baby Bear's chair had a really slippery transfer board to help him get from his wheelchair to his regular chair.

Upstairs, there were three beds. There was a great big bed for Papa Bear,

a middle-sized bed for Mama Bear,

and a special bed that moved up and down for Baby Bear.

One morning, Mama Bear made some porridge for breakfast. She filled a great big bowl for Papa Bear, a middle-sized bowl for herself, and a wee little bowl for Baby Bear.

The porridge was too hot to eat, so Mama Bear and Papa Bear decided to take Baby Bear to physical therapy while the porridge cooled off.

At the Treetop Center, Baby Bear works with the physical therapist and physical therapist assistant. They are helping Baby Bear's muscles get stronger by doing special exercises with him.

That same morning, a little girl named Goldilocks was walking through the forest. She came to the three bears' house and knocked on the door to see if anyone was home. No one answered, but the door opened easily, so she peeked inside.

When Goldilocks saw the three chairs, she invited herself into the bears' home. She sat in the great big chair, but it was too hard. She sat in the middle-sized chair, but it was too soft. She sat in the wee little chair and it was just right, until it broke!

Goldilocks got up from the floor and saw the porridge sitting on the table. "I'm hungry," she said. She tasted the porridge. The porridge in the big bowl was too hot. The porridge in the middle-sized bowl was too cold. The porridge in the wee little bowl was just right, so she ate it all up.

Now Goldilocks was tired.
She walked up the ramp to the bedrooms
and tried the beds. The great big bed was too
hard. The middle-sized bed was too soft.

The wee little bed was just right. It had a
remote control to make it go up and down and
everything! Goldilocks lowered the bed, jumped
in, and gave herself rides up and down until
she fell asleep.

Baby Bear was finished at physical therapy, so the three bears headed home.
Papa Bear and Mama Bear took turns racing Baby Bear in his wheelchair as they
ran through the forest.

The moment they got home, they knew someone had been there.

"Humph," said Papa Bear in his great big voice, "someone has been sitting in my chair."

"Land sakes," said Mama Bear in her middle-sized voice, "someone has been sitting in my chair."

"Oh dear," cried Baby Bear in his wee little voice, "someone has been sitting in my chair and they broke it all to bits!"

Then they all looked at the table.
"Humph," said Papa Bear in his great big voice,
"someone has been tasting my porridge."

"Land sakes," said Mama Bear in her
middle-sized voice, "someone has been tasting
my porridge."

"Oh dear," cried Baby Bear in his wee
little voice, "someone has been tasting my
porridge and they ate it all up!"

Then Papa Bear, Mama Bear, and Baby Bear all went up the ramp to the bedrooms.

"Humph," said Papa Bear in his great big voice, "someone has been sleeping in my bed."

"Land sakes," said Mama Bear in her middle-sized voice, "someone has been sleeping in my bed."

"Oh dear," cried Baby Bear in his wee little voice, "someone has been sleeping in my bed…

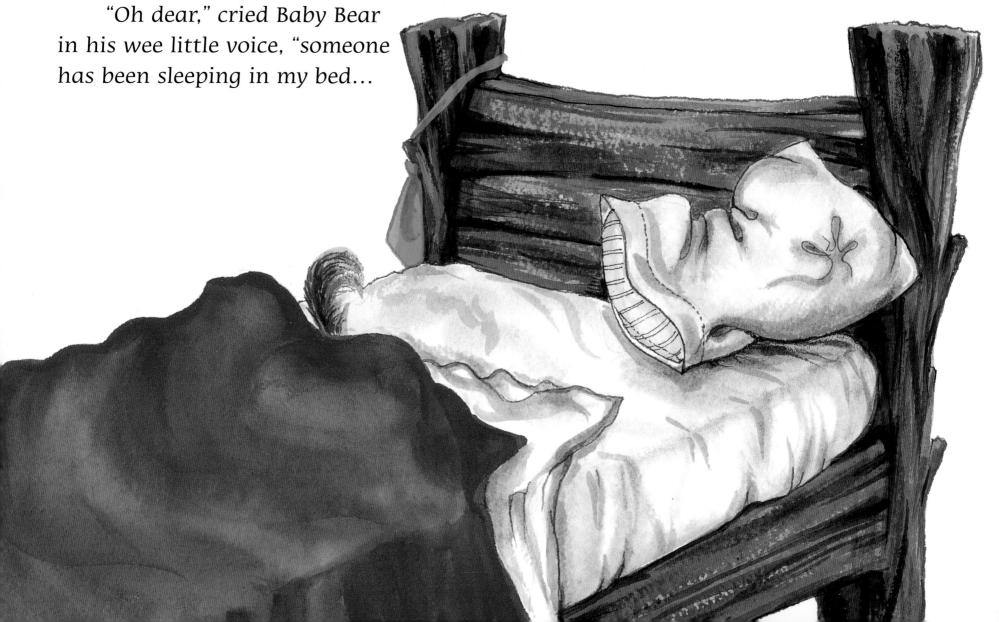

...and she is still here!!"

Goldilocks opened her eyes and saw the three bears.
"Yikes!" she said. She was very frightened at the
sight of the three bears.

Baby Bear could see that she was afraid, and gently asked, "Why were you in my bed?"

Goldilocks said, "I was lost, hungry, and tired when I found your house in the forest. I knocked on the door, but no one answered. The door was open, so I came in."

Baby Bear felt sorry for Goldilocks. He said, "I will help you find your way back home."

"Thanks," Goldilocks said. "I think your bed is pretty neat." Then she asked Baby Bear questions about his wheelchair. She had never seen one before.

Baby Bear explained, "The wheelchair helps me to get around . . . Would you like a ride?"

Baby Bear's wheelchair was just right for Goldilocks. She fit perfectly! Goldilocks tried to move around the room in the chair, but her arms got very tired.

Baby Bear said, "I used to get tired too, before I started going to physical therapy. Now I don't get so tired."

From that day on, Baby Bear and Goldilocks were the best of friends and they played all kinds of games together. When Baby Bear got tired, Goldilocks offered to push his chair for him. Sometimes he said yes, and sometimes he just said no.

Both Goldilocks and Baby Bear had made a
friend for life and they lived happily ever after.

The End!